Contents

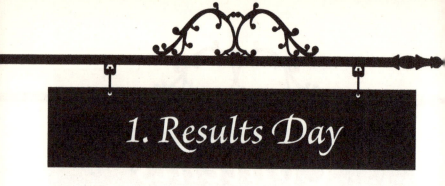

1. Results Day

"Bills, bills, bills," says Mum, sorting through a pile of post. "It's always bills – or people trying to sell us things!"

I'm sitting in the kitchen with my little brother Ocean, my mum and her girlfriend Josie. It was Ocean's birthday last week. Since then, he's hardly stopped looking at his favourite present – a book of weird facts about London – and reading them out loud to us.

"Did you know that there are so many trees in London that it's officially a forest?" he says.

"Um, no," I say. "But that's cool."

I'm distracted by the delicious-looking pastries on the table. They are a treat for Josie's twin teenage daughters, Iona and Ella, who are getting their exam results today.

Hideaway Hotel
Marathon Magic

Written by Sarah Hagger-Holt
Illustrated by Beatriz Castro

Hachette UK's policy is to use papers that are natural, renewable and recyclable products and made from wood grown in well-managed forests and other controlled sources. The logging and manufacturing processes are expected to conform to the environmental regulations of the country of origin.

ISBN: 978 1 3983 7718 9

Text © Sarah Hagger-Holt
Illustrations, design and layout © Hodder & Stoughton Limited
First published in 2023 by Hodder & Stoughton Limited (for its Hodder Education imprint, part of the Hodder Education Group),
An Hachette UK Company
Carmelite House, 50 Victoria Embankment, London EC4Y 0DZ

www.hoddereducation.com

Impression number 10 9 8 7 6 5 4 3 2 1
Year 2027 2026 2025 2024 2023

Author: Sarah Hagger-Holt
Series Editor: Catherine Coe
Commissioning Editor: Hamish Baxter
Illustrator: Beatriz Castro / Advocate Art
Educational Reviewer: Pauline Allen
Design and page layouts: Rocket Design (East Anglia) Ltd
Cover design: Julie Joubinaux
Editorial: Estelle Lloyd, Amy Tyrer

With thanks to the schools that took part in the development of *Reading Planet KS2*, including: Ancaster CE Primary School, Ancaster; Downsway Primary School, Reading; Ferry Lane Primary School, London; Foxborough Primary School, Slough; Griffin Park Primary School, Blackburn; St Barnabas CE First & Middle School, Pershore; Tranmoor Primary School, Doncaster; and Wilton CE Primary School, Wilton.

A catalogue record for this title is available from the British Library.

Printed in the UK.

Orders: Please contact Hachette UK Distribution, Hely Hutchinson Centre, Milton Road, Didcot, Oxfordshire, OX11 7HH.
Telephone: +44 (0)1235 400555. Email: primary@hachette.co.uk.

MIX
Paper | Supporting
responsible forestry
FSC™ C104740

We all live together, along with Josie's older son Dan, in a tiny flat at the top of Hideaway Hotel. Josie will take the twins into school today to pick up their exam results, while Mum looks after the hotel.

"Oh look, Skye," says Mum to me. "There's some post for you too!"

I eagerly take the postcard. It's from Liam, one of my best friends. I thought he might have so much fun on holiday that he'd forget all about me. But he hasn't.

Hi Skye,
We won! We came joint first in the talent show at the caravan park! The other winner was a girl telling jokes too. Amazing!

She taught me this:

What can run but has no legs?
A nose!

Ha ha.

See you soon!
Liam

Skye Piercy

Hideaway Hotel

Expedition Road

London WC1

£1.35

Liam had been so excited about entering the talent show with his cousin Luke. It's brilliant that they won. But I wish I could have been there. Instead, I'm stuck at Hideaway Hotel. We're not going on holiday because Mum and Josie have to work all summer.

Iona appears. She's very pale. She slumps at the table.

"Have a pastry," says Josie, pushing the plate towards her. "They're your favourites."

"Ugh," shudders Iona. "I can't eat anything. I'm too stressed."

"Iona, did you know that there used to be a polar bear in the Tower of London?" says Ocean, looking up eagerly from his book.

"Not now, Ocean," she replies. "I'm not in the mood for facts. Even ones about polar bears."

Ella bounces into the kitchen, grabs a pastry and takes an enormous bite.

Iona glares at her. "It's all right for you," she mutters to her twin. "You're really good at exams."

Josie squeezes Iona's hand. "Whatever happens, the most important thing is that you both did your best."

"Huh," grunts Iona.

"Ella …" says Ocean.

"Go on, what's today's fun fact then?" replies Ella. Ocean beams at her and flicks through the book.

"Did you know that the first London Marathon was the only one to have two winners? They were called …" he trails off – the words are too long for him to read by himself.

Ella leans over and finishes the sentence for him. "Dick Beardsley and Inge Simonsen, in 1981. Thanks, Ocean, I'm sure that will come in handy!"

"Let's go," says Iona anxiously. "We don't want to be late."

After they've gone, Mum goes to work. Ocean runs off to find Dan and tell him facts about London.

"I've got a really good one," he says. "About this bus that jumped over Tower Bridge ..."

Now it's just me left in the kitchen.

It's boring sitting by myself, so I decide to go exploring. I'm not really allowed to go in the guest corridors, but it's quiet today, so hopefully no one will notice me.

I know which room I want to visit. I helped Mum and Josie to decorate it, just before the hotel opened a few weeks ago. It feels like my own special place. Whenever I go in there, and climb into the window seat, something strange and wonderful happens.

I grab a pastry from the plate and head to Room 14. I'm ready for an adventure.

2. Running Scared

I curl up on the window seat, nibbling my pastry while I wait for the magic to work. I didn't believe in magic until the first time I hid here. Now I know it's true. Each time I come to Room 14, I travel back in time! But I don't know if it will happen today.

When I can't wait any longer, I push back the curtains and …

There's a boy sitting on the floor outside the bathroom door, staring at it like he could open it with the power of his mind if he tried hard enough.

"Come on," he says to the closed door. "Please, Emma, just come out."

There's muffled sobbing from behind the bathroom door.

The boy places his hands on the door. "Please! It's not long before it starts. You've been training so hard. You don't really want to miss it, do you?"

There's a loud sniff. "I don't care," says a girl's voice from inside the bathroom. "I'm not going. Mum and Dad can't make me. Neither can you."

The boy looks round the room, as if searching for ideas. He catches sight of me and jumps up in surprise. "Where did you come from?" he demands.

"I ... er ... I work at the hotel," I say.

"You don't look old enough to work here. You're not even wearing work clothes," he continues, looking at me doubtfully. "Anyway, you should have knocked."

"Sorry," I say. "My mum owns the hotel, so sometimes I help out here." He seems to accept this.

"Davey, who's that?" interrupts the voice from the bathroom. "Is it Mum and Dad again? I've told them, I'm not coming out!"

Davey rolls his eyes at the door.

"You know the London Marathon?" he whispers.

"Course I do," I whisper back. "It happens every year. It's huge. Thousands of runners come from all over the world."

He looks at me like I've said something odd. "Not *every* year," he corrects me. "There's never been a marathon in London until today. My big sister, Emma, is supposed to be running in it. Except she's locked herself in the bathroom and won't come out. I don't know what to do."

Oops! I should have learnt by now not to say anything that makes me sound weird. This is the third time that Room 14 has magically sent me shuttling back in time. I don't think Davey suspects there's anything strange about me though – he's too busy worrying about his sister.

"Mum and Dad couldn't get her to come out, so they asked me to try," says Davey. "But she won't budge." His face lights up. "Hey, if you work here, maybe you have a key?"

"I don't have a key," I say. "But I have got an idea. Give me a minute."

I let myself out of Room 14, and dash down the corridor to the cleaners' cupboard. I grab some cleaning spray and a cloth.

I'm in such a hurry that I don't look where I'm going. I almost crash into a man standing in the doorway of Room 15. He's wearing striped pyjamas and his hair's standing up on end. He looks worried.

"Sorry!" I say.

"My alarm clock didn't work," he says, in an accent that I don't recognise. "Do you know what time it is?"

I quickly glance at my watch. "Seven o'clock," I tell him.

"Oh, what a relief," he says. "I still have plenty of time. Thank you." And he disappears back into his room.

Back in Room 14, I rap on the bathroom door. "Hello?" I say. "I'm here to clean the bathroom. Can you let me in?"

"Come back later!" Emma says.

"See what I mean?" whispers Davey.

I try again. "You don't have to come out, just let me in. I'll get into trouble if I can't do my job." It's not true, but it might persuade Davey's sister to open the door.

There's a pause, a shuffle, then the lock slides back.

Davey gives me a thumbs up. It feels like the two of us are on the same team.

Emma is sitting on the floor, her head in her hands. She looks as pale as Iona did at breakfast.

"You can't be here to clean the room! You're just a kid," she says. I hold up the cleaning materials to show her. She nods, but she's got a faraway look on her face.

"Why are you hiding in here?" I ask, sitting down next to her.

"Ohhhh," she wails. "I feel sick. I want to run today, I really do. But the race is so big, and all the other runners are so much older and faster than me. What if I do really badly or I have to drop out before the finish? If I don't take part, then I can't mess it up."

I remember what Josie said to Iona this morning. "You just have to try your best," I tell Emma. "Your family will be cheering you on. They don't mind how fast you run, they just want you to have fun."

I hope that's true. I've only just met Davey, and I've never met their mum and dad. That's what Mum and Josie would say, but there are some pushy parents out there who might pile on the pressure.

"My family are brilliant," Emma says. "But they are so excited about me taking part in the marathon that I don't think they'd understand if I told them I was scared." I hand Emma a piece of loo roll and she blows her nose loudly.

"It's okay to be scared," I say. "I bet even some of the fastest, most experienced runners are feeling nervous right now. But please don't give up before you've even started."

Emma looks at me thoughtfully. I think she might be ready to come out of the bathroom. I hope Davey doesn't come barging in. I bet he's listening at the door. I would be if I were him.

But he isn't. He must have gone to find his mum and dad because the three of them burst into Room 14, just as I open the bathroom door.

Emma's parents give her a big hug.

"I'm sorry, I'm ready now," she says, pulling away. "Let's go!"

"Thank you," Davey says to me. "I don't know how you did that. You must be magic or something!"

"Magic, ha ha," I say. If only he knew.

"We have to go now. Will you come with us to watch the race?" he asks.

"Yes please," I reply eagerly.

"You'd be very welcome!" chuckles Davey's dad, shaking my hand so hard that I think it might fall off. "You've saved the day! If it wasn't for you, Emma would still be hiding in the bathroom. You're like a lucky charm." He laughs with a big booming laugh.

I cross my fingers for Emma, and for my own big sisters, Iona and Ella, back home. If I *am* a lucky charm, like Davey's dad says, I reckon they'll need some good luck today as well.

"We need to hurry! It's past eight o'clock now," explains Davey, as we leave the hotel.

I look at my watch, surprised. How can it be that late already? But my watch still says seven o'clock. It must be broken. Maybe it couldn't cope with the strain of time travel!

Oh no, that means I must have told the man in Room 15 the wrong time. But there's no time to go back now. Davey and his family are already halfway to the bus stop.

When I time-travelled before, my clothes changed into uncomfortable old-fashioned outfits. So I'm glad, as I sprint after them, that 1980s shorts and T-shirts are as easy to run in as my normal clothes.

When we get to the stop, Davey, Emma and I leap onto the open back of the bus. We're out of breath and laughing. Davey's mum and dad grab onto the rail and pull themselves on board behind us, just as the bus is picking up speed.

It's too noisy to talk much, but Davey and I keep grinning at each other. We cross over the Thames, and eventually stop right by the park. I'm so excited to be on an adventure with a new friend.

3. Race Against Time

We have to squeeze through the crowds to get to the runners' area at the start line.

There are people everywhere – jostling each other, jogging on the spot or doing stretches. Some are laughing and joking. Others look deadly serious. Everyone is here for the same reason. It's incredibly exciting. I feel my tummy fluttering with nerves – and I'm not even running!

Emma hugs her parents and her brother. Next, she turns to me and gives me a hug too.

"Thank you," she whispers in my ear. "I'm still scared, but that doesn't matter. I'm going to run anyway."

"Good luck!" calls Davey after her. He's bouncing up and down with excitement.

"Wow, it's really happening," he says to me. "There are 7,000 runners here – and my sister's one of them! The best runners have come from all over the world for this race. In fact, guess what?"

"What?" I ask.

"Some of them are staying in your hotel," Davey says, excitedly. "Dad said that Dick Beardsley's staying downstairs, and Inge Simonsen, the one from Norway, he's in the room opposite us. Neither of them has won a marathon before, but either could win today. That's what Emma's running magazine says. We saw Simonsen in the corridor yesterday. When he found out that Emma was running, he gave her his autograph and wished her luck. He said he'd see us today."

"He's staying in Room 15?" I ask, picturing a man with messy hair and striped pyjamas.

"That's right. Why? What's wrong? You look like you've seen a ghost!"

I don't know what to say. I can't give away that I know the result already: Dick Beardsley and Inge Simonsen will be joint winners.

Except ... will they? What if Simonsen doesn't even make it to the race, because I told him the wrong time? It would be awful if he missed his chance to win and to make history.

If Simonsen doesn't race, then that will change what happened in the past. What if I've changed the whole course of history, for everyone? It could affect loads of other things in the present or in the future! It could mean that I can't time-travel back home, or that if I do, everything there will be different. It would be all my fault. I feel sick just thinking about it.

"Can you see him?" I ask Davey. We've managed to squeeze into a great viewing spot, just by the start line, where the elite runners are warming up.

"I'm not sure ... not yet ..."

The crowd is enormous and it's hard to see anything as people keep moving around. We have to be careful not to get squashed. So many people have come for a day out, to catch a glimpse of something completely new – this special race that's taking place in London for the first time ever.

"Hop on my back," I say. "Then you'll be able to see better."

Davey peers at the runners. "No," he says finally. "That's odd, isn't it? I hope he's on his way. He's cutting it fine." Davey jumps down from my back.

There's no point looking at my watch – it's still broken – but clearly the race will start soon. I don't think Simonsen's going to make it.

I've messed this up. But now I've got to put it right.

"Sorry," I say to Davey. "I've got to go back to the hotel right now. It's an emergency." He looks at me open-mouthed, but I don't have time to explain.

I push through the crowds towards the park gates. I don't think I've ever run so fast! I'm out of breath by the time I reach the bus stop.

I wait, panting. Even if I do find Simonsen at the hotel, we might not make it back before the race starts. But I've got to try.

The roads are busy. The sound of cars honking their horns is overwhelming. Minutes tick by. I can't see a single bus. This is getting worse and worse.

Suddenly, I hear a voice next to me, breathing heavily.

"I didn't think I'd catch you up. You're really fast, you know?" Davey says.

"What are you doing here?" I ask.

"I wanted to help," he says. "Just like you helped us earlier. I've told Mum and Dad I'm with you and we'll meet them later at the park."

"Oh," I wail. "I'm useless, I'm no help at all. In fact, I just make things worse." I tell him what happened with Simonsen, although nothing about how worried I am about changing history, of course!

"You're not useless," says Davey. "You're going to sort it out. It will be okay." I wish I believed him.

A black taxi stops at a red light in front of us. Despite living in London all my life, I've never been in one. Mum says they're too expensive. But they look so glamorous that I've always wanted to. Taking a taxi might be our only chance to get to the hotel in time.

I rummage in my pockets, but they are empty.

"Davey, do you have any money?" I ask him hopefully.

"Only a few pence and my bus ticket," he says. "And a chocolate bar ... but it's a bit squashed."

"Well, let's try," I say, trying to sound more confident than I feel. "We can get some money at the hotel and pay the driver when we get there."

Nervously, I knock on the window. The driver lets us in.

When the door shuts, the traffic noise vanishes. Davey and I sit on the black leather seats and stretch out our legs. It's like stepping into a private world, just like when I hide behind the curtains in Room 14.

"Where to, love?" asks the driver through the glass that separates us. Her voice is brisk, but kind.

I feel embarrassed, but I have to say this. "I'm sorry … er … we don't have any money … but …"

She interrupts me with a smile. "It's alright, love, this journey will be free. You're my first fare, see, I've only just qualified. It's a London taxi tradition that the first passenger for every new driver goes free."

I stare at her in surprise. At last, some good luck! I give her the hotel address and glance at the clock on the dashboard. We've not got long till the race starts.

"Please go quickly," I say, as the taxi pulls away. "It's an emergency."

"Half the roads are shut because of this wretched marathon," she exclaims. "The traffic's terrible. But I'll go as fast as I can. Just hold on to your hat, okay?"

I'm about to tell her that I don't have a hat, when the taxi speeds off.

We weave through the cars and buses, making sharp turns down back streets and hurtling back over the bridge.

After only a few minutes, she screeches to a stop. She was so fast. I feel like cheering. I would never have guessed that we were her first ever customers. She knew all the shortcuts without using a map or a sat nav.

I start to imagine myself behind the wheel of my own shiny cab. Driving a taxi would be such an amazing job, far more fun than running a hotel!

"I thought you were in a rush!" she says. "Go on, scarper, I've got work to do."

"Thank you!" Davey and I shout, as we run towards the hotel, up the stairs, down the corridor, and knock on the door of Room 15.

We wait. No one answers.

"Maybe he's already gone?" suggests Davey. "That would be good, right? He's probably on his way ... or perhaps he's already there."

I shake my head. "Listen! There's music coming from the room. Someone's in there. He just can't hear us."

We pound on the door. "Mr Simonsen!" I shout, and Davey joins in.

Finally, the door opens. Inge Simonsen is standing there in his running kit with his race number on his shirt.

"Who is it?" he says, sounding annoyed. Then, he sees Davey and smiles. "Ah, my little friend with the running sister. There's no time for another autograph now, I have to leave for the marathon. I was just listening to my lucky song. I can't be late."

"I'm sorry," I say. "You already are. It's nearly nine o'clock."

Simonsen looks shocked. "You can't be serious! It's much earlier than that!"

"I'm afraid not," I say. "I'm so sorry, I made a mistake. I told you the wrong time before. We have to go right now."

Simonsen looks bewildered as we bustle him out of his room and down the stairs. Halfway down, I realise his music is still playing, but there's no time to turn it off.

"How will we get there?" he asks. "I don't know London very well."

"Neither do I," says Davey.

They both look at me. I look at the road. The traffic is gridlocked. We're going to have to find another way.

"Let's head towards the river," I say. "Then at least we're going in the right direction."

I'm sure Simonsen would be faster without us, but he doesn't know where he's going. Anyway, it's my fault that he's late, and my fault if history gets changed, so *I* need to sort it out.

"What's that?" asks Davey. "It looks like a spaceship."

I sigh. There's no time to point out the tourist attractions!

"That's the entrance to a tunnel under the Thames," I tell him. "It's a shortcut to Greenwich for walkers and cyclists."

"Greenwich?" asks Davey. "You mean where the marathon starts?"

Of course! I drag them both towards the tunnel entrance. Ahead of us are three men carrying bikes on their shoulders down the stairs.

At the bottom, one of them notices Simonsen's running number.

"On your way to the marathon?" he asks us.

"Yes," I say. "But we're late and he's going to miss the start and then he won't win the race and it's all my fault and ..." I'm breathless and nearly crying. We're never going to make it. "I don't suppose you could help us somehow?"

The cyclist looks concerned. He whispers to his friends, then turns back to us.

"We can offer you a lift," he says. "It's not elegant, but it is speedy. Hop on the back of our bikes and take our spare helmets. We'll get you through the tunnel as fast as we can pedal."

We each perch behind one of the riders. I hold on tight and screw my eyes shut as we zoom along. I open them for a split second, and see Davey on the next bike, beaming at me. He's having an amazing time, but I still feel sick with worry.

At the end of the tunnel, we hop off. The cyclists wave and shout, "Good luck!".

"It's too late," I say to Davey gloomily. "The race has started."

"It might have started," Davey says. "But we're not too late."

"That's right," says Simonsen. "I've missed my spot at the front with the other fastest runners, but I can still join the race at the back and catch up. That cycle ride really got me warmed up and ready to go!"

"... And ready to win!" I shout. He puts his thumb up at us as he disappears among the other runners.

"Look!" says Davey, waving and jumping up and down. "It's Emma. And there's Mum and Dad." We have arrived just at the right moment to watch Emma cross the start line.

I can't relax yet. Yes, Simonsen's in the race. But my mistake might still mean that he doesn't win. I might still have changed history.

Davey's parents get us all hot chocolate. We catch the bus to the finish line, but hop off a couple of stops early to watch the runners.

I can feel rain trickling down my back, but I don't mind the bad weather. No one seems to be bothered either – they are just excited to be here. Runners pour down the road in front of us. It's like watching a river of people flow past. They look unstoppable, but I wonder if they will all make it to the end of the race.

Davey and I join in the clapping and cheering, shouting out the numbers of the runners who go past. Some of them smile and wave at us. But I'm impatient to get to the finish and see if the result I'm expecting to happen actually does.

5. Hand in Hand

"He's coming!" shouts Davey, leaning forward against the barrier.

I peer round him anxiously. Two runners are sprinting towards the finish tape. And one of them has familiar messy hair. "You mean, *they're* coming," I say. Can I dare to believe that it's all going to be okay?

Both runners are straining ahead, panting, their faces grimly determined. Imagine still being able to run that fast after 26 miles! It feels like the whole crowd is holding its breath to see who will win.

Simonsen and Beardsley hold hands and run in perfect rhythm to the finish line. Despite their tiredness, they smile and hold up their joined hands. The crowd cheers.

Thank goodness, I didn't change history after all! Simonsen and Beardsley are the winners of the first London Marathon, and I was here to see it.

Davey grabs my hand and we both jump up and down. Not just one winner, but two! No one expected that to happen. No one, except me.

More runners are crossing the line now, but we know we will have to wait a long time before Emma comes. At last, I can relax and enjoy the race.

"Hey, look!" Davey shouts, after what feels like ages. "It's Emma! Come on, sis!"

Emma looks exhausted, but she's still running. We shout and whoop as she gets closer.

All of a sudden, she cries out. I lean over the barrier to see what's happened. Emma's on the ground, clutching her ankle.

"Em, are you okay?" Davey shouts from behind the barrier. "Can you move?"

"Ow, it hurts so much," moans Emma. She's blinking back tears. "I'll never finish the race now. I've trained so hard for nothing."

"Don't give up now!" I shout from the sidelines. "You're so close."

She heaves herself up. She's wincing in pain, but she finds the strength to hobble towards the finish. It's only a few metres, but it seems to take forever.

Everyone is cheering. Davey's mum and dad shout loudest of all. The cheering grows as Emma slowly crosses the finish line.

Emma sits down on the kerb, while a first-aider checks her ankle. She has a finishers' medal around her neck.

"Well done!" bellows Davey's dad.

"Really?" says Emma. "That wasn't the way I wanted to finish."

"But you finished. You didn't give up." He waves his camera at Emma. "Let's have a photo of you with your medal."

"I'll take the photo," I say quickly. "Then you can all be in it."

"But what about you?" Davey asks me.

I shake my head. I'm not sure it's a good idea for someone from the future to be photographed in the past. I've nearly changed history once already today, I don't want to take any more risks!

"Hello there," says a familiar voice behind me. "It's my friends from the hotel. We meet again!"

I turn round. It's Simonsen. I worry that he might be annoyed about the mess we got him into earlier, but he's smiling broadly.

"Well done!" says Davey. "We saw you and Dick Beardsley cross the line together."

"Thank you." He turns to Emma. "Was that your first marathon?" She nods. "Well done, maybe I'll see you running again next year. Although, next year, I hope there'll be a bit less drama for all of us!" He winks at me and Davey.

"Excuse me," says Davey's dad. "Would you mind joining our photo?"

Simonsen, Davey, Emma, and their mum and dad all crowd together.

"Smile!" I say. They all do. The two medals sparkle in the flash from the camera.

London 1981

6. Running Home

Davey's dad has a Polaroid camera where the photo prints out straightaway. When the first image pops out, Davey's mum gives it to me.

"Take this as a memory of today," she says. "Now, let's all get back to the hotel. Emma must be tired." She turns to me. "Won't your parents be worrying about you?"

Oh no. I've been away for ages. It's been great to celebrate with Davey's family, but now I want to see my own family again. Hopefully there will be more celebrations now that Ella and Iona have got their results! I need to get back to the window seat in Room 14 before the magic can take me home.

But this time Room 14 won't be empty and waiting for me. Davey and his family will be there. How will I sneak on to the window seat without them noticing? What will they think if I suddenly disappear? Maybe the magic won't work if someone else is in the room. What will I do then?

On the bus back to the hotel, Davey chatters on, but I'm too busy worrying about whether or not I'll be able to get back to Mum and Josie. As soon as the bus slows down, I leap to my feet.

"Goodbye," I say quickly.

"But ..." stutters Davey. "You're not running away again?"

"Sorry!" I say, and leap off the back of the bus.

I imagine that I'm a marathon runner, powering towards the finish line. I sprint down the street, and up the steps to the front door. I race past the other rooms to the familiar door of Room 14.

In the window seat, I shut my eyes. I hope that Davey and his family don't burst into the room and interrupt the magic before it can work. I feel really tired and my legs ache. It's so comfortable. I lean back and ...

I wake up with a jolt. How could I have fallen asleep? I pull open the curtains and, to my relief, the room is empty, just like it was when I sneaked in after breakfast.

When I get back to the flat, Mum, Josie, Iona and Ella are sitting round the kitchen table. They are all talking and laughing. Ocean is sitting on Mum's lap, slurping his fruit juice. I'm surprised to see Mum and Josie in the same place – usually they are both busy around the hotel. I guess they must have got Dan to cover reception.

"Skye, where have you been?" says Mum.

"Nowhere much," I say, hiding the marathon photo in my pocket.

"Are you ready for the good news?" Mum asks. I nod eagerly.

"We did it!" chorus Iona and Ella. I jump up and give them both a big hug.

"Well, she did much better than me," says Iona. "As usual!"

"We both got the grades to go to college!" adds Ella. "Come on, Iona, we need to get ready." She tugs at her sister's hand. "We're off to celebrate with our friends!" They whirl out of the kitchen, giggling together.

Mum turns to me. "I bet you miss your friends, Skye," she says. "It must be boring for you, hanging round the hotel by yourself."

At the start of the summer, I thought it would be boring. But my adventures in Room 14 have meant that I've hardly had time to be bored.

"Liam and Farida will be back soon," I say. *I'll have so much to tell them*, I think to myself, *that I won't even know where to begin.*

Now answer the questions ...

1 What was Ocean's fun fact about the first London Marathon?

2 Why did Skye feel as if she and Davey were on the same team on page 14?

3 'Maybe it couldn't cope with the strain of time travel!' (page 17). Can you think of a word that could be used instead of 'strain' in this sentence?

4 What happened when Skye found out she'd told Inge Simonsen the wrong time earlier that day?

5 What did you think might happen when Skye and Davey went back to find Inge Simonsen?

6 The taxi driver told Skye: "Half the roads are shut because of this wretched marathon." How does the word 'wretched' add to the meaning of the sentence?

7 Why did Skye imagine she was a marathon runner on page 43?

8 If you could travel to any time in history in the place where you live, when would you choose and why?